Kiana's
Iditarod

Kiana's Iditarod

Manufactured in China by C&C Offset Printing Co. Ltd. Shenzhen, Guangdong Province in November 2017

ISBN 13: 978-0-934007-07-8 / ISBN 10: 0-934007-07-1 (hardcover)
ISBN 13: 978-0-934007-00-9 / ISBN 10: 0-934007-00-4 (1st paperback edition)
ISBN 13: 978-1-57061-589-4 / ISBN 10: 1-57061-589-6 (2nd paperback edition)

PAWS IV
Published by Sasquatch Books
1904 Third Avenue, Suite 710
Seattle, Washington 98101
(206) 467-4300
www.sasquatchbooks.com

Kiana's Iditarod

By SHELLEY GILL   Illustrated by SHANNON CARTWRIGHT

Kiana's
Iditarod

is dedicated to the brave lead dogs of Alaska.

Samson . . .

killed by wolves at Colorado Creek in 1979. He was a strong dog; too slow for an Iditarod team, but brave when the end came.

And of course Nugget, Tekla, Beaver, Harvey, Dandy, Cora Gray, Wilbur, Rabbit, Duke, Jody and the rest.

Iditarod

The Iditarod Race began simply; Alaskans Joe Redington Sr. and neighbor Dorothy Page thought racing across 1000 miles of tundra, mountains and moose might be a fun idea.

Other folks, the rugged Alaskan types, agreed. Since then, 1974, the Iditarod has become a world renowned event, complete with television, cheechako groupies and enough rules and regulations for three races. But the Iditarod was such a good idea it has even survived its own publicity and remains, true to its name, "The Last Great Race."

To run to Nome a driver needs a leader like Kiana; smart and bred to break trail. Unlike the lost souls of the show ring, Iditarod dogs are bred for good feet, a fast trot, happy dispositions and voracious appetites. If a dog has those qualities a driver doesn't care what she looks like.

An Iditarod team goes into training in October and works hard right up until race time in March. Each driver tries to work out a secret diet that will give his dogs the edge. Beaver, beef, moose and fish are measured into the dog pot each morning and night.

A few weeks before the race, drivers put together their 'drops:' burlap bags stuffed full of dog food, booties, extra socks and batteries, candy bars and trail dinners. These are flown to the checkpoints along the trail and dropped from bush planes.

Each driver must sign in and out of each checkpoint. Failure to do so means disqualification. Each driver must have an axe, enough booties for each dog, enough food for himself and the team, snowshoes, a parka, and an Arctic sleeping bag.

Nights on the trail can get mighty cold with wind chill factors dropping the temperature to 100 below. Yet most nights are spent out on the trail. Villages are often too noisy and the wise driver will move his team on a few miles before making camp. Then both he and his dogs can get some rest.

The Iditarod is run along a turn-of-the-century gold rush trail. The original trail ran from Seward to Nome. Today the Iditarod National Historic Trail stretches from Anchorage to Nome. The race covers two different routes. The trail described in this book follows the Yukon River through Ruby, Galena and Nulato. The northern route fights a bitter wind into the ghost town of Iditarod then turns up river to Anvik, Grayling and Eagle Island. The number one position in every Iditarod is reserved for the legendary Leonhard Seppala, an Alaskan dog musher who was part of the relay team that took diptheria serum by dogteam to Nome in 1925 and saved the town from an epidemic.

Anyone who finishes the race will remember their days on the trail for the rest of their lives but the real heroes of the Iditarod are the lead dogs. A good leader can feel a trail with the pads of her feet. She takes her commands immediately but, in a crunch, she will do the right thing even when her driver is yelling at her to do the opposite. A leader like Kiana will take her team straight into a bitter storm rather than turn, and with the wind at her back, lead them out to sea.

The Iditarod; a race that's run
a thousand miles to Nome.
A husky named Kiana,
who made the trail her home.
A man, a team, Alaska bred,
adventure was their creed.
They would struggle 'til
the bitter end,
to claim this mighty deed.

*T*he birch dipped icy spears of light,
to dance upon the scene.
The morning of the last great race,
the dog lot was serene.
The sled was packed, the runners sharp,
the harnesses dry and clean.
Atop their houses the huskies lay,
breathing frosty puffs of steam.

The trucks were parked in the early light,
   on the ice of Settler's Bay.
Howls and yips filled the air;
   for months they had trained for this day

The man lifted Kiana down from the dog box,
   where she had slept snug in the straw.
"We could've been last," he said with a grin,
   "but first is a tough place to draw."

*T*he young husky leader
  leaned hard in her traces,
eager to be on her way.
  But the man checked each harness
and petted each dog,
  until finally he reached for the sleigh.

"Five, Four, Three, Two, One!"
the man shouted "Hike!"
And Kiana pulled hard
for her stride.
Beyond stretched the trail
a thousand miles long
silent, lonely, untried.

Twenty-six checkpoints
  lay somewhere ahead.
A mountain range or two.
  There were moose
    and wolves
    and nights so cold,
    they'd turn your mittens blue.

On the frozen Yentna River,
   they stopped to make first camp.
The dogs slept warm, while the man chopped wood,
   by the light of a miner's lamp.

              The miles fell long
                 behind them.
              Skwentna passed dark
                 in the night.
              Still Kiana pressed on,
                 bred to run,
                 the motion was sheer delight.

W hen they plunged down the cliff
   at Happy River,
a moose stood smack
   in the trail.
"Whoa," yelled the man
   as he fired two shots,
and that deadly beast
   turned tail.

The spruce trees stood
    as sentinels,
on the shores of
    Pontilla Lake.
Guarding the trail
    toward Rainy Pass,
that the dogs and
the drivers would take.

The air was
crisp and silent;
the snow was drifted deep.
And the mushers
    spoke in whispers,
    hoping the peace
    would keep.

They started the climb
  after four hours rest;
up to a sea
  of endless white.
In bitter cold
  they reached the top,
a moonscape
  bathed in light.

Rohn River cabin
was a welcome sight,
as the dogs struggled down
the pass that night.
A 24-hour layover was
the rule of the race.
And the Rohn was the
ideal resting place.

Next morning Kiana woke and stretched
  to chase her dreams away
She eyed a stranger in another team,
  then scampered over to play.

But the big McKenzie husky lunged;
  his chain rang taut in the cold;
His teeth were bared, his anger deep;
  no pup should be so bold.

Stiff-legged, Kiana held her ground,
  young though she might be.
A leader's blood and pride were hers,
  this brute would surely see.

They circled then;
  one fast and lean,
  the other old and strong.
The McKenzie was the first to break,
  admitting he was wrong.

At breakfast Kiana
  shared her meat.
They romped throughout the day.
  As the Northern Lights streaked
  across a midnight sky,
curled together
  the huskies lay.

A t noon they pulled into Farewell,
200 miles from home.
Weak dogs were loaded
on bush planes;
worn out, they would
never reach Nome.

School was out early
in Nikolai.
Children scampered
to meet the teams.
March was the month
for dog racing.
When Iditarod filled
their dreams.

*Four hours on, four
  hours off.
Rest when the sun
  is high.
Eat, then sleep, then
  hit the trail,
or faster teams pass
  you by.*

*The Tokotna winds
  past McGrath.
That night it was
  forty below.
Bright cotton booties
  Kiana wore,
as she splashed
  through the overflow.*

The coffee was hot
in Ophir.
Eight drivers slept
hard on the floor.
When one man moved
the others stirred,
they kept one eye
peeled to the door.

It was a gold rush
 trail they traveled next day;
past towns long covered with dust.
 Poorman, Cripple, Ruby and Long;
Roadhouses abandoned to rust.

Down the mighty Yukon
 they raced,
as the slower teams fell
 behind.
The man fed them
 broth,
and doctored their feet.
He was tireless, tender
 and kind.

Galena was past,
  Nulato ahead,
when the wolves
  slid out of the brush.
The Call of the Wild
  sang on the wind,
as the team surged ahead
  with a rush.

*I*nside the checkpoint
    at Kaltag,
weary mushers plotted
    and schemed.
When the fire died to
    coals they finally slept.
But "the trail" was the
    stage for their dreams.

At Unalakleet the teams
    turned east,
onto the ice of
    Norton Sound.
The houses at Shaktoolik
    fought the wind,
with cables set deep
    in the ground.

Out on the ice
   Kiana was lost.
She didn't know which
   way to go.
The trail was gone,
   the sky was white
buried by raging snow.

All around her head
   it swirled,
her muscles screamed
   in pain,
every step back was
   a moment lost,
a foot the storm
   had gained.

Then up ahead a stake
   appeared,
solid in the ice.
Kiana knew the trail
   was found,
but the team had
   paid a price.

Exhausted and frozen
   they stumbled along,
   till nighttime greyed to dawn.
Beyond the checkpoint
   at Koyuk,
only nine dogs would
   push on.

*I*cebergs blue and frosty,
  sparkled like glass in the sun.
As they rounded the
  cliffs near Elim,
Kiana broke into a run.

Fifty teams were behind
  them,
Four more for Kiana
  to catch.
Two hundred dogs
  had gone back home.
Six teams had been
  forced to scratch

In White Mountain
   the old women met them,
with berries and
   caribou meat.
They left while two
   teams were still sleeping,
the snow quiet beneath
   their feet.

The three teams raced
in single file,
as the sun dipped
low in the west.
It was now or never,
win or lose.
Could Kiana prove
she was the best?

The other mushers drove
  with headlamp aglow,
while the man preferred
  the night.
So Kiana crept by in
  the shadows of dark,
out of the range
  of their light.

W

hen they were past,
  she heard the man yell.
    And a crowd began to cheer.
Her weary feet picked-up the pace,
  as the finish line drew near.
Her canine heart swelled with pride;
  it was a gallant thing she'd done.
As they crossed beneath
  the famous arch,
Kiana's race was won.

*T*he End

Glossary

Alaska Range - Crescent shaped mountain range which includes Mt. McKinley.

Booties - usually made of canvas, they are worn like socks to protect the dogs' feet.

Broth - tired dogs sometimes get dehydrated so mushers cook them broth; usually with a bit of beaver or fish meat thrown in for flavor.

Bunny boots - white rubber boots that will keep your feet warm down to 40 below.

Checkers - volunteers who man the checkpoints and keep tabs on drivers and dogs.

Checkpoint - There are usually between 25 & 26 official checkpoints. Some are gracious homes; others are rough tent camps. They are the "mileposts" of the race where drivers check in and pause to rest and sip a cup of coffee. They are also where drivers can drop off a tired dog or perhaps call home with the help of the volunteer ham radio operators who ensure the safety of drivers and dogs.

Dog pot - Usually a lightweight aluminum aviation gas can that drivers use to cook their dog food in.

Gangline - the main line that stretches between dogs and is hooked to the sled.

Gee - the command for the leader to turn the team right.

Harness - usually custom made of nylon with a pile padding.

Haw - the command for the leader to turn the team left.

Kuspuk - An Eskimo pullover parka usually made of calico with a squirrel lining.

Mukluks - Eskimo footwear.

Overflow - the water that flows on top of a heavy layer of ice in very cold weather.

Picket line - a cable used to stake out your dogs at night.

Restart - the Iditarod Race officially starts in Anchorage and has a restart at Knik on Settler's Bay.

Runners - are the strips of wood, metal, ivory or plastic attached to the bottom pieces of the sled. Iditarod racers prefer high pressure plastic that glides smoothly.

Ruff - The fur sewn around the hood of a parka. The best is wolverine because it frosts less than wolf or coyote.

Sleigh - a musher's term for his sled.

Swing - the dogs that run directly behind the leader and are part of the "front end" of the team.

Stakes - The Iditarod trail is marked with stakes, reflectors and tripods.

Training - Iditarod racers must begin training for the March race in October when the first snow falls. They will drive their team up to 80 miles a day as race time nears so both dog and musher will be prepared for the rigors of the trail.

Wheel dogs - the dogs who run directly in front of the sled. These must be your strongest team members.

Whoa - Stop!

THE ALASKA ABC BOOK

KIANA'S IDITAROD

MAMMOTH MAGIC

ALASKA MOTHER GOOSE

THUNDERFEET

DANGER – The Dog Yard Cat

ALASKA'S THREE BEARS

NORTH COUNTRY CHRISTMAS

COUNT ALASKA'S COLORS

IDITAROD CURRICULUM

SWIMMER

DENALI CURRICULUM

ADVENTURE AT THE BOTTOM OF THE WORLD

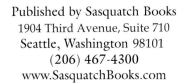
STORM RUN

Titles available from PAWS IV

Published by Sasquatch Books
1904 Third Avenue, Suite 710
Seattle, Washington 98101
(206) 467-4300
www.SasquatchBooks.com

PAWS IV VIDEO COLLECTION